Sometimes I Feel Sad

Tom Alexander

Sometimes I feel sad.

Sometimes it's because
I've lost something.

Or because I'm hurt.

Other times I don't know why I feel sad.

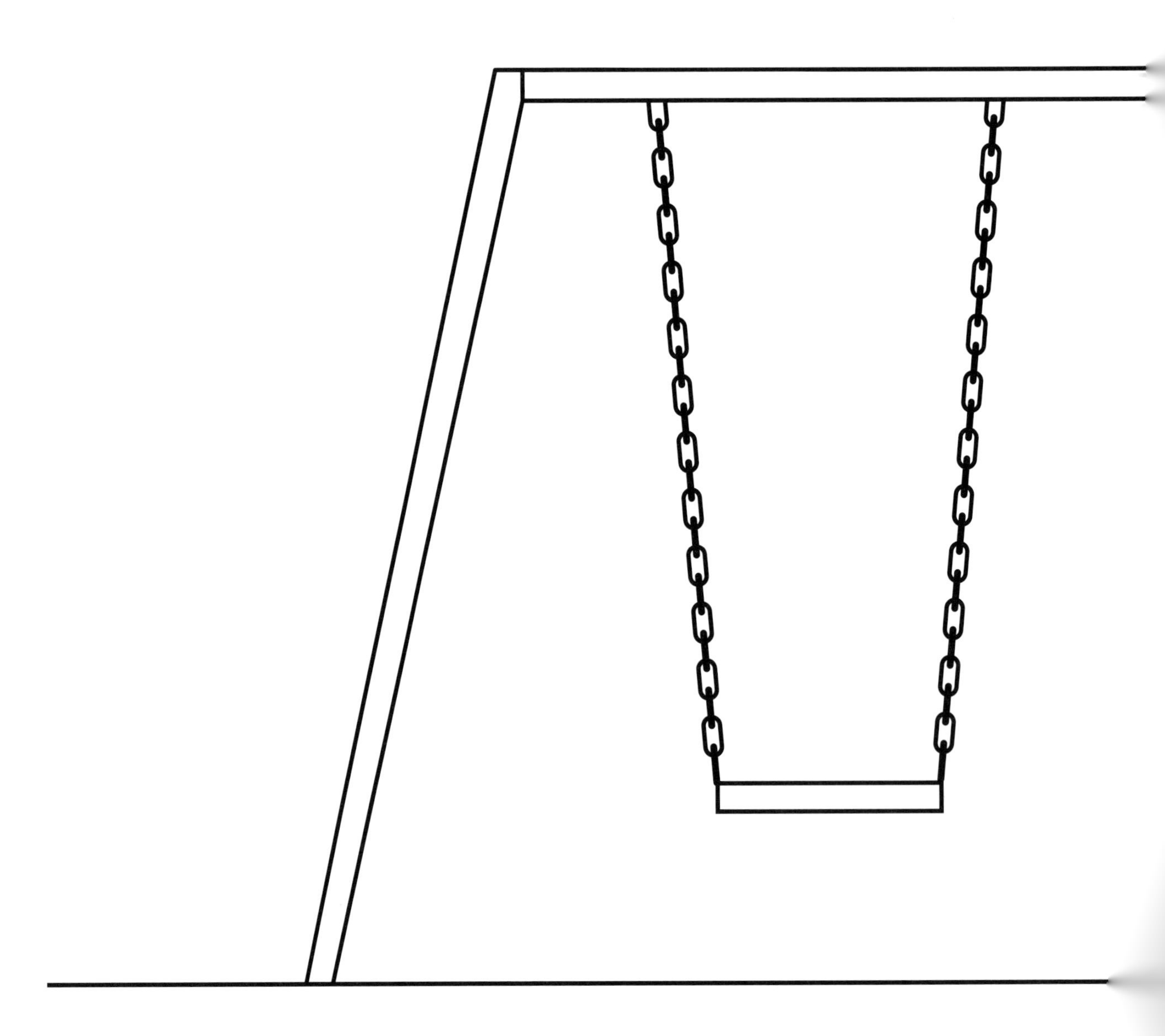

I just do.

Sometimes being around other people helps.

Sometimes it doesn't.

Sometimes doing something fun cheers me up.

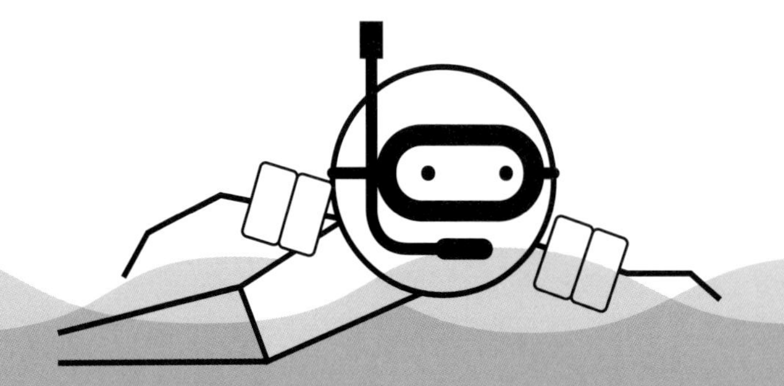

Sometimes it just makes me feel sadder.

Sometimes being by myself
helps the sadness go away.

Sometimes it just
makes it worse.

When I feel sad, it can be difficult to let other people know.

Like my friends.

Or my parents.

Or my teacher.

I worry about what they will think of me.

Or that I'll make them sad, too.

It can be scary to tell people
how you really feel.

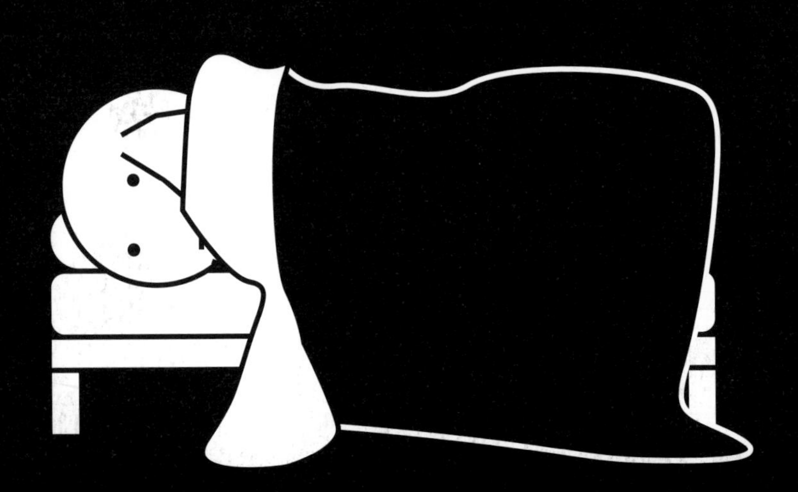

But telling people is the only way to make it better.

Some people don't pay attention.

Or they don't believe me.

Others tell me just to cheer up.

Or try not to think about it.

Those things don't help.

I wish they did.

So I keep trying until someone listens.
Someone who understands.

They tell me it's OK to feel sad sometimes.

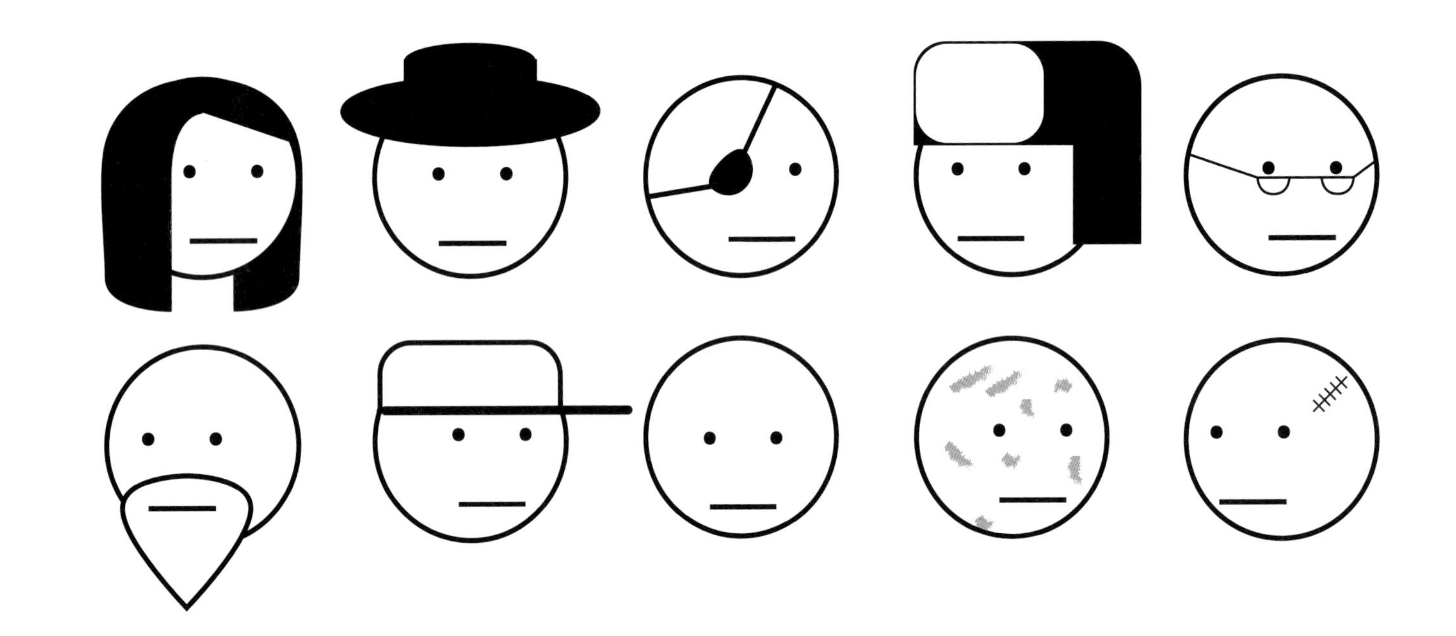

Everybody does.

That makes me feel a bit better.

Because it means I'm not alone.

First published in 2018
by Jessica Kingsley Publishers
73 Collier Street
London N1 9BE, UK
and
400 Market Street, Suite 400
Philadelphia, PA 19106, USA

www.jkp.com

Library of Congress Cataloging in Publication Data
A CIP catalog record for this book is available from the Library of Congress

British Library Cataloguing in Publication Data
A CIP catalogue record for this book is available from the British Library

ISBN 978 1 78592 493 4
eISBN 978 1 78450 889 0

Printed and bound in Great Britain by Bell and Bain Ltd, Glasgow

My Secret Dog

Tom Alexander

I always wanted a dog, but
Mum said I wasn't allowed.
So I got one anyway.
My secret dog lives in the
cupboard and we sneak out
at night to play.
We'll be best friends forever.
As long as Mum doesn't
find out...

Tom Alexander writes stories, draws pictures and makes weird little things out of paper. He lives in London with his wife and cat.

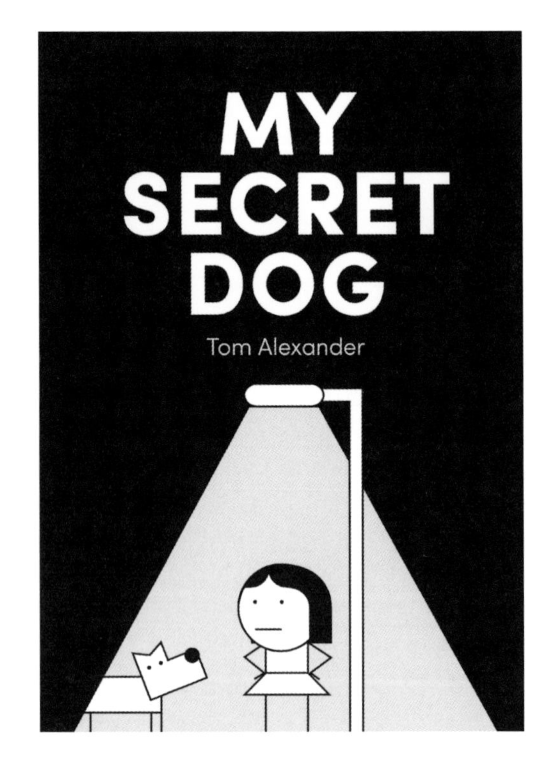

Hardback | £9.99 | $15.95 | 40 pages
ISBN-978 1 78592 486 6 | eISBN-978 1 78450 874 6